P9-BYJ-822

DATE			

BAKER & TAYLOR

WICKED JACK

ADAPTED BY

CONNIE NORDHIELM WOOLDRIDGE

ILLUSTRATED BY WILL HILLENBRAND

HOLIDAY HOUSE/NEW YORK

There're goings-on across the Great Dismal Swamp of Virginia and North Carolina that are mighty hard to explain. But I can tell you one thing: the mysterious light you see dancing around out there of an evening is because of Jack — Wicked Jack.

Old Jack was a blacksmith, but the thing he really took pride in was his meanness. He talked so bad to people, they steered clear of him 'cept when they had to have a tool fixed or a horseshoe made.

This was worrisome to Jack. You see, without enough folks to practice his meanness on, he was afraid he'd get rusty at it.

So he hit on a plan. He would invite a stranger in for some vittles.
Then, after the poor fellow had a good mouthful
of greens or cornbread, Jack would commence with his meanness.

One day an old crippled-up man passed by the house. Jack had to carry him up the dirt path, the man was so bent over. When the vittles were on the table, the stranger couldn't even feed himself. Jack had to do it for him.

"This is an awful lot of bother just to practice my meanness," Jack thought. There was a flash of light, and the crippled-up stranger disappeared. Before Jack's popped-out eyes sat a man—old and white-bearded but straight as a poker—wearing a white robe with a key dangling from his waist.

"Who in thunder are you?" Jack demanded.

"I'm Saint Peter, the keeper of the heavenly gate," said the old man. "And you, Jack, are meaner than a rattlesnake. But you behaved right hospitable to me today so I'm going to give you three wishes as a reward."

Jack rubbed his prickly chin and figured he had nothing to lose by playing along. After some hard thinking, he said, "The first thing I wish is that any old loafer who sits in my rocker'll stick tight to the chair bottom. He'll keep a-rocking and a-rocking till he yells for me to let him go."

"Next thing I wish," said Jack, "is that anybody who touches my sledgehammer'll stick to it like glue while it hammers this a-way and that a-way. It'll throw him around till he hollers for me to let him go."

"And last," said Jack, "I wish that anybody who touches the firebush in front of my shop'll get pulled right into the middle. He'll stick there in the prickles till he shouts for me to let him go!"

"I guess that does it, Jack," Saint Peter said, a-scribbling away in a little white book.
"But I don't mind saying those are three of the
sorriest wishes I ever did hear of!" Then he up and disappeared.

After that Jack got meaner than ever.

It wasn't long before the Devil was worried that Jack was outdoing even him for meanness. So he sent one of his boys — a sawed-off little devil with horns just beginning to sprout — to fetch old Jack before he was dead. That little devil strutted into Jack's shop like he meant business.

"Daddy sent me after you," he said, "so you just better come on with me!"

"Why, sure," said Jack. "Just let me finish this horseshoe and I'll be right along."

The little devil sat down in Jack's rocking chair—real cocky-like—to wait for Jack to finish the horseshoe. Soon as he settled himself in, that chair began to rock like there was no tomorrow. The little devil stuck to it like glue with his horned head going WHACK-A-BANG, WHACK-A-BANG against the back of it.

"Hey! Let me up out of this chair!" he hollered.

"You gonna hightail it out of here if I let you up?"

"Sure, Mister!" (WHACK-A-BANG, WHACK-A-BANG.)
"Just let me up!"

"All right then, get on out of here!" said Jack. The rocking
chair threw the little devil to the floor. He scrambled to his feet
and with Jack's help was out the door and down the road.

Jack was having himself a good laugh when another one of the Devil's boys came a-strutting into the shop — a little bigger devil with horns an inch or two high.

"My daddy sent me to fetch you so you
better come along RIGHT NOW!"

"Why, sure," said Jack. "One more good
bang and this horseshoe'll be finished. Just
hand me my sledgehammer. Or is it a mite
too big for a young whippersnapper like you?"

"Nothing's too big for me!" bragged the medium-sized devil, and he took hold of the hammer. Soon as he did, it began to throw him all over the shop — up, down, this a-way, and that a-way till he was begging Jack to turn him loose.

"You ever fixin' to come back here again?" Jack asked him.

"Not me, Mister!" answered the medium-sized devil, still flying all over the shop.

"Not you nor that little brother of yours?"

"No, Mister! Neither one of us'll ever come back here again!
Just turn me loose!"

"All right then!" said Jack, and the medium-sized devil
fell—SPLAT!—on the floor. He was out of the shop and down
the road as fast as his legs could carry him.

Old Jack had hardly got all the laugh out of *that* one when into the shop walked the old Devil himself. His horns stuck way out the top of his head, his tail was a-twitching, and he was so mad there was smoke coming out of his ears.

"Well, howdy do," said Jack.

"Don't you 'howdy do' me, Old Man! I don't like how you done my boys, so I come for you myself! Now, you come on along!"

"If you'd just care to have a sit in my rocking chair— —"

"I don't care to sit in any chair of yours!"

"Well then, if you'd just hand me my sledgehammer — —"

"No, I'm not handing you any sledgehammer! Now you just come on!"

"Well all right then, I'll come. There's no sense getting yourself so worked up! Let's you and me just walk on out the door!"

This suited the Devil just fine except that right outside the door, Jack gave him a little nudge that made him brush up against the firebush growing out there.

Lickety-split, there was the Devil stuck in the middle of the firebush with his head down in the prickles and his feet sticking out the top. Jack sat down on a tree stump and began picking dirt out from under his fingernails.

The devil thrashed and kicked and flailed but the more he did, the more prickled and stuck he got. So finally, he just grew real still.

"Mister?"

"What you want?"

"Let me out of here."

"Now why would I want to do a fool thing like that?"

"Because if you do I'll never bother you again —not me nor my boys."
Jack just kept picking at the dirt under his fingernails.

"Mister...please?"

Well, this was too much for Jack, hearing the Devil himself say "Please" so pretty, and he laughed till he didn't have another laugh left in him. When he finally caught his breath, he said, "All right then, get on out of here! And don't you go fooling with Wicked Jack again!"

The Devil took off, and folks on down the road who saw him pass say he wasn't moving slow!

After that, Jack just kept getting older
and meaner till finally he up and died.
The first place he headed for was the pearly
gate of Heaven and gave a knock.
BAM! BAM! BAM!

Saint Peter opened the gate a
crack. "What're you doing
here, Jack?"

"I'm here to join the celestial
kingdom," Jack answered in his
very best preacher-like voice.

"Nobody comes in here, Jack, unless his name's written in The Book. Your name's not there, 'cause I just checked this morning when I heard your time was up."

"You can't turn me down after I come all this way!"

"Jack, I know my business!" said Saint Peter, and he closed the gate up tight.

There was nothing for Jack to do but turn around and head the other direction. He walked and he walked till he saw the gates of Hell standing wide open like the jaws of a hungry mountain lion. Pretty soon he got so close he could make out the Devil's two boys playing catch with a ball of fire.

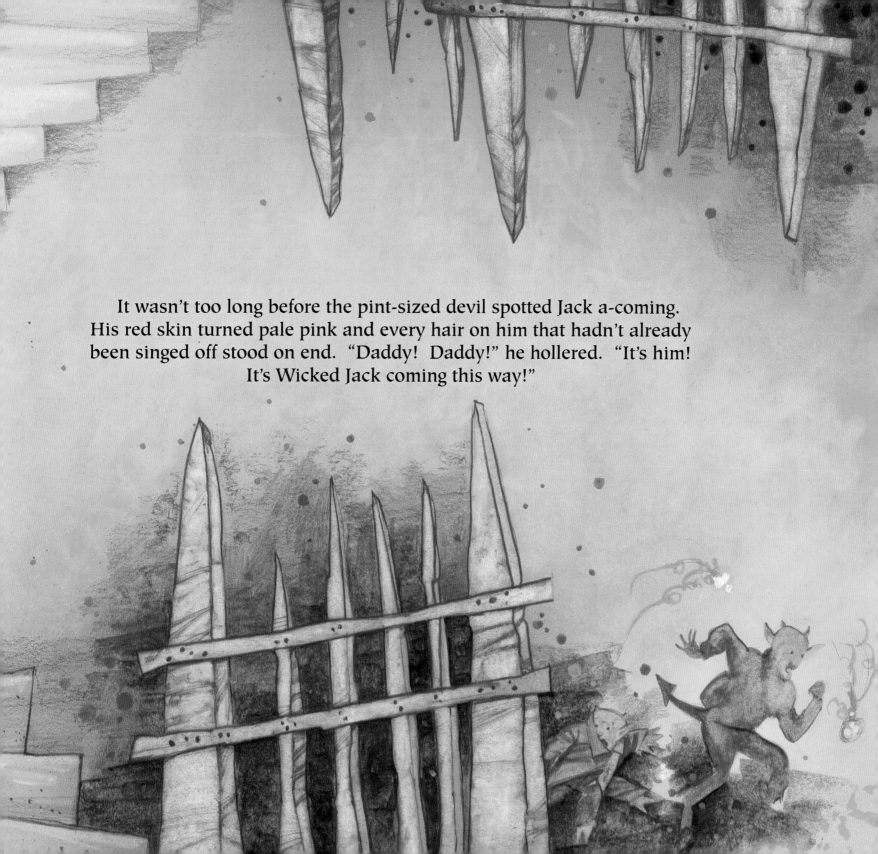

It wasn't too long before the pint-sized devil spotted Jack a-coming. His red skin turned pale pink and every hair on him that hadn't already been singed off stood on end. "Daddy! Daddy!" he hollered. "It's him! It's Wicked Jack coming this way!"

The Devil came running. "Shut the gates, boys!" he barked. "And fetch me a hot coal with these here tongs!" The pint-sized devil shut the gates while his brother fetched his daddy a hot coal. "You can't come in here, Jack! Uh-uh!"

"But I already been turned away up yonder!"

"That's no affair of mine! Now you git on out of here!"

"And just what am I supposed to do now?"

"I'll tell you what you do, Jack. You take this here coal," and he passed the tongs out the bars to Jack, "and you go start yourself a hell of your own!"

There hasn't been a body before nor since turned down up above
and down below. And the light out over the swamp? Well, the scientific
folk'll tell you it's marsh gas. But you and I know it's just old Wicked Jack
a-wandering to and fro with his coal.

AUTHOR'S NOTE   Part of the fun of folktales is digging around to find as many different
retellings as possible. My adaptation of "Wicked Jack" is based on two versions by Richard
Chase, "Wicked John and the Devil" in *American Folk Tales and Songs* (Dover, 1971) and
Wicked John and the Devil (Houghton Mifflin, 1951), and one by Zora Neale Hurston in
Mules and Men (Lippincott, 1935).

ARTIST'S NOTE   The artwork for this book was done with graphite on paper
with oil, oil pastels, and a smudge of the coal left over from the illustrator's jack-o'-lantern.

—————◆—————

To the five delightfully disorganized people with whom I share my life—
Carl, Christina, Scott, Sean, and Eric—and to
Donna Dryden, who tries valiantly to bring some order into our chaos.
—C.N.W.

To David, who first heard this story on a ride down Spooky Hollow Road.
—W.H.

—————◆—————

Text copyright © 1995 by Connie Nordhielm Wooldridge
Illustrations copyright © 1995 by Will Hillenbrand
All rights reserved
Printed in the United States of America
First Edition
Type design by Will Hillenbrand

Library of Congress Cataloging-in-Publication Data
Wooldridge, Connie Nordhielm.
Wicked Jack / adapted by Connie Nordhielm Wooldridge;
illustrated by Will Hillenbrand. — 1st ed.
p.   cm.
Summary: A mean old blacksmith's actions leave him unwelcomed
by both Saint Peter and the Devil when he dies.
ISBN 0-8234-1101-X
[1. Folklore—United States.] I. Hillenbrand, Will, ill.
II. Title.
PZ8. 1.W8724Wi 1995
398.21—dc20
[E]

93-13248
CIP AC